Batter Royale

by Leisl Adams

AMULET BOOKS · NEW YORK

Library of Congress Cataloging Number
for the hardcover edition: 2021941588

Hardcover ISBN 978-1-4197-5075-5
Paperback ISBN 978-1-4197-5076-2

Text and illustrations copyright © 2022 Leisl Adams
Colors by Andrew Dalhouse
Book design by Andrea Miller

Printed and bound in China
10 9 8 7 6 5 4 3

Amulet Books are available at special discounts when purchased in quantity for premiums and promotions as well as fundraising or educational use. Special editions can also be created to specification. For details, contact specialsales@abramsbooks.com or the address below.

Amulet Books® is a registered trademark of Harry N. Abrams, Inc.

ABRAMS The Art of Books
195 Broadway, New York, NY 10007
abramsbooks.com

To my dad, who said,
if anyone could do it, you can

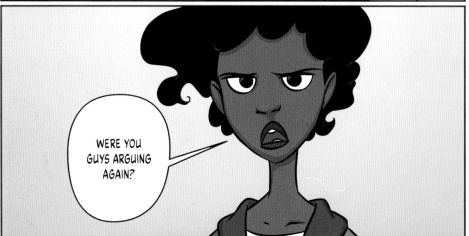

WERE YOU GUYS ARGUING AGAIN?

NO! NO! NOT AT ALL!

WE WERE JUST TALKING, HON!

3

APPLE Crumble

SERVES 1

 1 apple, peeled, cored, and chopped

 1 teaspoon orange or lemon juice

1 tablespoon butter

FOR THE Filling

1 teaspoon brown sugar

¼ teaspoon cinnamon

water (optional): add 1 teaspoon at a time to make a sauce

Directions

1. Preheat oven to 350°F. Prepare a ramekin or oven-safe bowl with cooking spray or butter.

2. Place all ingredients in a pan on medium heat. Cook for 5 minutes or until apples are soft.

FOR THE Topping

¼ cup flour

¼ cup quick oats

2 tablespoons softened butter

½ teaspoon cinnamon

¼ cup brown sugar

1. Place all ingredients in a medium bowl. Using a fork, mash all ingredients together until crumbly.

2. Transfer cooked apples to buttered and floured bowl or ramekin.

3. Add crumble mixture to top. Bake for 20 minutes.

TIPS

- Get fancy by adding ice cream, whipped cream, or caramel!
- You can experiment with different apples for different flavors and textures! I like McIntosh best!

SIGH

LATE AGAIN, ROSE?

SORRY, MA'AM!

APPLY TO ANY COLLEGES YET?

JUST ONE ACTUALLY. I DON'T KNOW IF I CAN AFFORD IT THOUGH.

HAHA, REALLY? I'VE APPLIED TO LIKE, FIVE!

HEY, FRED!

OH, HEY, UH . . . HOW YA DOIN'?

GOOD. YOU?

I'M OKAY. MUM'S JUST CALLED A MEETING FOR THE KITCHEN STAFF. I THINK SHE'S LETTING A FEW PEOPLE GO . . . SHE CAN'T AFFORD TO KEEP THEM.

AT THIS RATE I'LL BE STUCK HERE FOREVER.

OOOH, DO YOU THINK SHE COULD USE SOME HELP WITH FOOD PREP?

YOU COULD GIVE IT A SHOT!

15

GIGGLE

SO, WHAT ARE YOU DOING AFTER SCHOOL IS OVER?

CHOCOLATE Truffles

¼ cup cream cheese

¼ cup chocolate baking crumbs

1 tablespoon powdered sugar

2 tablespoons cocoa powder

sea salt (for finishing)

1 cup chocolate, melted

Directions

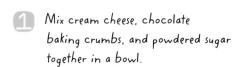

1. Mix cream cheese, chocolate baking crumbs, and powdered sugar together in a bowl.

2. Roll approximately 1 teaspoon of the mixture at a time into individual balls.

3. Cover in cocoa powder or melted chocolate and sea salt, then refrigerate until ready to serve.

½ cup
chocolate chips

½ heavy
whipping cream

Directions

1. Place ingredients in a microwave-safe bowl.

2. Microwave in 20-seconds increments until chocolate chips start to melt.

4. Once cooled, use a hand or stand mixer to whip until stiff peaks form.

3. Whisk until combined, then refrigerate mix until cool.

5. Spoon into individual bowls or glasses.

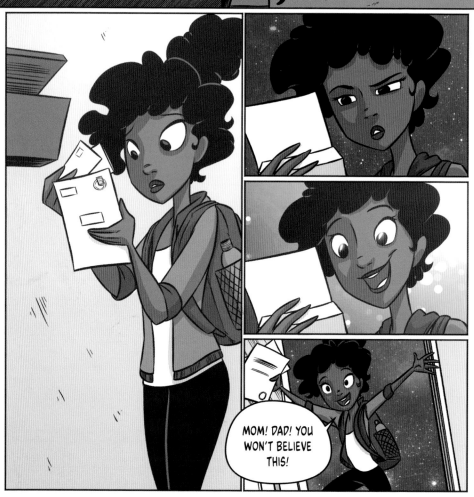

MOM! DAD! YOU WON'T BELIEVE THIS!

27

I KNOW WE SHOULD'VE BEEN HELPING TO CLEAN UP, AND IT WAS MY FAULT BECAUSE I WANTED TO TRY MY HAND AT MAKING SOMETHING IN THE KITCHEN AND WE SORTA LOST TRACK OF TIME AND I'M REALLY, REALLY SORRY AND I PROMISE TO BE MORE PROFESSIONAL IN THE FUTURE—

ROSE!

I **UNDERSTAND**!

I **KNOW** YOU WANT TO BE IN THE KITCHEN!

YOU AND FRED HAVE BEEN FRIENDS SINCE YOU WERE KIDS, BUT HE'S BEEN IN THIS KITCHEN HIS WHOLE LIFE, AND YOU'VE ONLY JUST STARTED.

I BELIEVE YOU CAN DO IT, BUT I NEED YOU TO BE MORE RESPONSIBLE! NO MORE ARRIVING LATE, AND NO MORE COOKING AFTER HOURS WITHOUT PERMISSION.

YOU'RE MY BEST SERVER. FOR NOW, I NEED YOU TO STAY OUT FRONT. LEARN THE ROPES! THERE'S MORE TO RUNNING A KITCHEN THAN JUST COOKING.

OKAY, CHEF!

34

UM, ROSE? YOU'RE MAKING THAT WEIRD FACE YOU ALWAYS MAKE WHEN YOU COME UP WITH A BAD IDEA.

WHAT IF WE **ADDED** A *NEW* DESSERT FOR HER TO SAMPLE? I KNOW WHAT SHE'LL **LOVE!**

WHAT? **NO!**

ARE YOU KIDDING? THIS ISN'T A GAME; THE RESTAURANT IS ALREADY IN ENOUGH TROUBLE AS IT IS!

OKAY! OKAY! I GET IT.

CRASH!

37

40

45

53

VANILLA STRAWBERRY
Shortcake

SERVES 8

²⁄₃ cup cold
butter, cubed

2 cups flour

1 teaspoon baking
powder

 FOR THE Cake

2 tablespoons
sugar

²⁄₃ cup
buttermilk

1 egg

Milk or egg
whites, for
brushing

Directions

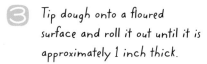

1. Preheat oven to 425°F. Place the cubed butter and flour into a bowl and cut together with a fork until mixture becomes crumbly.

2. Add the baking powder and sugar. Combine the buttermilk and egg in a separate container, then make a well in the center of the dry ingredients. Pour the wet ingredients into the well, then combine to form a dough.

3. Tip dough onto a floured surface and roll it out until it is approximately 1 inch thick.

4. Use a glass or round cutter to cut out round shapes. Transfer to a baking sheet and brush the tops with milk or egg whites.

5. Bake for 15 minutes or until golden.

FOR THE Strawberries

2 cups
strawberries

4 tablespoons
sugar

Directions

1. Remove tops from strawberries and slice (leave 4 or 5 whole). Place into a small bowl, coat with the sugar, and set aside.

1 cup heavy
whipping cream

½ teaspoon
vanilla

2 tablespoons
powdered sugar

½ teaspoon gelatin
powder (optional)

FOR THE Topping

Directions

1. If using gelatin, dissolve the gelatin powder in 1 tablespoon of hot water and set aside.

2. Using a hand blender or mixer with a whisk attachment, beat the heavy whipping cream on low, then slowly turn it up to medium speed. (Add the gelatin mixture as it thickens.)

3. Once the cream starts to hold its shape, add the vanilla and powdered sugar. Turn the speed to high and continue to whip until stiff peaks form.

 ASSEMBLY Assemble the cakes by cutting a scone in half and layering strawberries, then whipped cream inside. Place the other half of the scone on top and repeat the layers of strawberries and whipped cream. Place whole strawberries on top.

OH! HEY, ROSE! EVERYTHING OKAY?

UGH. MY PARENTS TOLD ME LAST NIGHT THAT THEY'RE SEPARATING. DAD WILL PROBABLY HAVE LEFT BY THE TIME I GET HOME.

I'M REALLY SORRY ROSE . . .

I'LL BE OKAY . . .

HAVE YOU GIVEN ANY MORE THOUGHT TO THE CONTEST?

ERM . . . I HAVEN'T REALLY THOUGHT ABOUT IT.

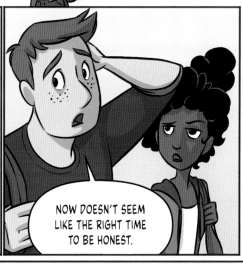

NOW DOESN'T SEEM LIKE THE RIGHT TIME TO BE HONEST.

I'D BETTER HEAD TO CLASS BEFORE I'M LATE.

YEAH, SEE YA.

BLUEBERRY Scones

MAKES 8 TO 10 SCONES

2 cups flour

1 tablespoon baking powder

½ teaspoon salt

2 tablespoons sugar

5 tablespoons cold butter

1 cup heavy whipping cream

1 cup frozen blueberries

milk or egg whites for the tops (optional)

Directions

1 Preheat oven to 400ºF degrees.

2 Whisk together flour, baking powder, salt, and sugar.

3 Cut butter into the flour mixture with a fork until it looks crumbly.

4 Fold in heavy whipping cream.

5 Turn the mixture out onto a floured surface.

6 Shape into a rectangle and fold in blueberries a bit at a time.

7 Once the blueberries are mixed in, roll into a rectangle again and cut into squares or wedges.

8 Place scones on a baking sheet and brush the tops with milk or egg whites, if using.

9 Bake for 15 to 20 minutes or until tops are golden brown.

OH! I FORGOT TO MENTION, YOU'LL HAVE TO LOOK OUT FOR TRAPS!

WHAT KIND OF CONTEST IS THIS??

WE JUST WANTED TO MAKE DESSERTS!

THEN MAYBE YOU SHOULD'VE STAYED HOME.

NICE WORK, NICOLE!

DO YOU KNOW WHY I CHOSE YOU?

IT'S BECAUSE YOU DON'T STAND A CHANCE, LOSERS.

POOF!

FOOM

SPLAT!

WHAT ARE YOU DOING? I THOUGHT WE WERE MAKING THE STRAWBERRY SHORTCAKE?

I THINK WE SHOULD DO SOMETHING NEW, YOU KNOW, TO IMPRESS SALLY!

WHAT? BUT THIS IS WHAT GOT US HERE!

TRUST ME!

48:09

ROSE?

OH, THAT LOOKS AMAZING!

HOW DO YOU GET THE PETALS SO THIN?

I USE THIS!

WHAT DO
WE DO?

SPLAT!

SUIT UP?

TIME'S UP!

TERRIBLE.
TOO DRY.

OH, COME **ON!**

CONSIDER YOURSELVES LUCKY.

CHOCOLATE STRAWBERRY
Shortcake

MAKES ONE

6-INCH CAKE

⅓ cup
self-rising flour

½ cup
all-purpose flour

½ teaspoon
baking soda

⅓ cup
cocoa powder

FOR THE
Cake

¾ cup
softened butter

¾ cup
sugar

1 teaspoon
vanilla extract

2 eggs

5 ounces
buttermilk

Directions

1 Preheat oven to 350ºF. Line a 6-inch cake pan with parchment.

2 Sift the self-rising and all-purpose flours and then combine in a medium bowl.

3 Add the baking soda and cocoa powder, then whisk together and set aside.

4 Cream together butter, sugar, and vanilla until fluffy. Add eggs, one at a time, until well combined.

5 Add the dry mix to the wet ingredients alternatively with the buttermilk, stirring until combined.

6 Pour into prepared cake pan. Bake for 50 minutes.

2 to 3 cups
strawberries

4 tablespoons
sugar

Directions

1. Remove tops from strawberries and slice (leave 4 or 5 whole). Place into a small bowl and coat with sugar and set aside.

 FOR THE
Topping

1 cup heavy
whipping cream

½ teaspoon
vanilla

2 tablespoons
powdered sugar

½ teaspoon gelatin
powder (optional)

Directions

1. If using gelatin, dissolve the gelatin powder in 1 tablespoon of hot water and set aside.

2. Using a hand blender or mixer with a whisk attachment, beat the heavy whipping cream on low, then slowly turn it up to medium speed. (Add the gelatin mixture as it thickens.)

3. Once the cream starts to hold its shape, add the vanilla and powdered sugar. Turn the speed to high and continue to whip until stiff peaks form.

 ASSEMBLY
When your cake is fully cooled, slice into two equal layers. On your bottom layer, spread a thin layer of whipped cream, then add cut strawberries and piped whipped cream on top. Place the other cake layer on top and repeat the layers of whipped cream and strawberries. Place whole strawberries on top.

 TIPS
○ Drizzle with melted chocolate or top with chocolate flakes.

COMING UP! THESE FIVE TEAMS WILL BATTLE IT OUT FOR THE TITLE OF BEST DESSERT CHEF . . .

. . . A BOOK DEAL, AND CASH PRIZE OF FIVE HUNDRED THOUSAND DOLLARS!

I REALLY WANT YOUR DESSERT TO BE AMAZING. MAKE ME FEEL SOMETHING!

OK, LET'S GO!

WE HAVE TO MOVE TOGETHER OR WE WON'T GET THROUGH THIS ROUND!

WHUMP!

SURPRISE INGREDIENT, LADIES AND GENTS!

BRUSSELS SPROUTS!

MAKE YOUR WAY OVER! AND DON'T FORGET, THIS INGREDIENT **MUST** BE FULLY INCORPORATED INTO YOUR CREATION!

WHAT THE HELL ARE WE GONNA DO WITH BRUSSELS SPROUTS?

I DUNNO . . .

MAYBE IF WE PUT IT INTO THE CRUST, IT'LL DISGUISE THE TASTE?

THAT COULD WORK.

NOW **THAT** IS A GREAT IDEA!

SO ROSE, WHAT'S IT LIKE WHERE YOU'RE FROM? COLD?

NO, NOT ALL THE TIME . . .

WELL, IT WAS NICE CHATTING WITH YOU!

WHIRRR

HMM, NOT BAD!

135

OH YEAH? I BET SHE'S THRILLED YOU'RE OUT HERE WITH ME INSTEAD OF WITH HER RIGHT NOW.

MAPLE CHOCOLATE CREAM CHEESE Tart

MAKES ONE 4-INCH TART

 FOR THE Crust

½ cup chocolate baking crumbs

3 tablespoons melted butter

Directions

1. Combine ingredients and pour into a 4-inch pan.

2. Use the bottom of a glass to press crust evenly to the bottom and up the sides.

3. Chill in the refrigerator while you make your filling.

1 tablespoon maple syrup

⅓ cup heavy whipping cream

½ cup cream cheese

¼ cup icing sugar

 FOR THE Filling

Directions

1. Using a hand mixer or stand mixer with a whisk attachment, whisk ingredients together until well blended.

FOR THE CHOCOLATE MAPLE **Glaze**

¼ cup maple syrup

⅛ cup cocoa powder

Directions

1. Combine ingredients in a small bowl.

2. Mix ingredients together until well blended. You can adjust the amount of cocoa or maple syrup depending on your taste.

ASSEMBLY Using a piping bag, pipe the filling onto the chocolate crust. Drizzle maple glaze on top.

○ Top with bacon crumble or a bacon slice!

TIPS

YOUR PARTNERS ARE ALL TIED IN THE CENTER, EACH WITH THEIR OWN LOCK.

FINISH THE RECIPE I PROVIDE **EXACTLY** AS IT'S WRITTEN, AND YOU WILL EARN THE KEY TO THEIR ESCAPE.

THE LAST ONE TO FINISH IS OUT OF THE COMPETITION. QUICKLY NOW, GET TO YOUR TABLES!

OKAY, I NEED TWO CUPS OF ALMOND FLOUR. GOT IT. EGG WHITES, CHECK.

AAAAAH!

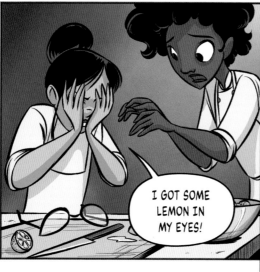

I GOT SOME LEMON IN MY EYES!

MFFMM!

Macarons

MAKES SHELLS FOR
15 to 20 **MACARONS**

 1 ½ cups icing sugar

 ⅔ cup almond flour

 3 egg whites

 3 tablespoons sugar

icing, ganache, or lemon curd (for filling)

Directions

1. Preheat oven to 325°F. Blend icing sugar and almond flour in a food processor and set aside.

2. With a hand mixer or stand mixer with a whisk attachment, whisk the egg whites until foamy. Add 1 tablespoon of sugar at a time, whisking until incorporated. Keep whisking until the egg whites get stiff and glossy.

3. Fold the almond flour mixture into the egg whites. The mixture should look smooth.

4. Fill a piping bag with the batter (I use a Wilton #12 tip) and pipe small rounds of batter onto a lined baking sheet.

5. Tap your baking sheet once or twice to work the air bubbles out.

6. Leave the cookies to dry for about 15 minutes. You can make sure they are dry enough by gently touching the surface. If your finger comes away clean, they're dry enough. The drier the better. Bake for 10 minutes.

7. Once fully cooled, spread half the cookies with icing, ganache, or lemon curd and top with the remaining cookies!

PINK PEONY

CONGRATULATIONS! YOU ARE THE FIRST TO MAKE IT BACK! ROSE AND FRED WIN THE ROUND!

YOU TRULY **ROSE** TO THE OCCASION! HAVE A DELICIOUS TIME ON THE LONDON EYE!

SHE'S ACTUALLY NOT AS MEAN AS YOU THINK, ONCE YOU GET TO KNOW HER . . . WELL . . . KINDA.

WAIT, ARE YOU JEALOUS?

HELL NO!

HEY, I'VE BEEN SERIOUS ABOUT WINNING THIS! YOU SAID YOU WERE TOO.

IT'S NOT *JUST* ABOUT THAT. . .

THEN WHY ARE YOU UPSET?

I GUESS, I'M UPSET ABOUT MY PARENTS SPLITTING UP. MAYBE I COULD'VE DONE MORE.

IT'S NOT YOUR FAULT.

SOURDOUGH ~ Starter

120 grams flour (use any kind but keep it consistent)

120 grams filtered water

Sourdough starter can be made in many different ways, but for this one you use equal weights of flour and water.

Directions

1. Stir flour and water together in a glass jar or bowl. Cover loosely and keep at room temperature or in an oven with the light on (don't forget that it's in there, like I did >.<).

2. Feed it once every twenty-four hours by discarding half of your mixture (120 grams) and adding a fresh 60 grams of flour and 60 grams of water.

3. After several days, the mixture should bubble and rise. Then you can feed it twice a day, every twelve hours. It may take several days or weeks of feeding before it's ready to use. You will know it is ready when it becomes very bubbly, with a dramatic rise in volume.

TIPS

You don't need to throw away the discarded starter! Keep it separately to use for pancakes, pizza crust, pretzels, and more! There are tons of recipes out there for sourdough discard!

DAMN!

EXCELLENT! NOW YOU HAVE A CHOICE . . .

PUSH THE SWITCH, AND CLOSE THE PIT SO EVERYONE CAN WALK THROUGH FREELY—

FLOUR

GREAT WORK TEAMS! WE'LL CONTINUE TOMORROW, WITH THE FINISHING OF OUR CAKES AND THE OFFICIAL TASTE TEST!

THE NEXT DAY:

GASP!

WHO WOULD DO THIS!

ALL RIGHT! WHO IS IT?

YOU! YOU DID THIS!

I WOULD NEVER—

AAAAAGH!

192

YEAST-BASED Cake

MAKES ONE 9-INCH CAKE

2 ¼ teaspoons yeast (or 1 cup sourdough starter)

¼ cup sugar

2 cups flour (1 cup flour if using sourdough starter)

½ teaspoon salt

FOR THE Cake

½ cup warm milk

2 eggs

4 tablespoons melted butter

Directions

1. Preheat oven to 400°F.

2. (If using yeast) Combine yeast with 1 teaspoon of sugar and ¼ cup of warm water and let stand for about 10 minutes.

3. In a separate bowl, combine flour, remaining sugar, and salt. Add yeast (or starter), milk, and eggs, and beat until combined.

5. Scrape down the sides of the bowl, cover, and let rise until doubled in size (approximately 45 minutes).

6. While the dough is rising, line a 9-inch cake pan with parchment paper.

4. Add butter and beat until smooth.

FOR THE Topping

¼ cup sugar

1 teaspoon cinnamon

2 tablespoons softened butter

Directions

1. In a small bowl, combine the ¼ cup of sugar and 1 teaspoon of cinnamon and mix.

2. Once risen, place the dough into the prepared cake pan and flatten down evenly. Spread the softened butter on the top, then sprinkle with the combined sugar and cinnamon.

3. Let rise for 15 more minutes. Bake for 25 minutes.

2 cups sugar

2 tablespoons melted butter

1 teaspoon vanilla

2 tablespoons milk

FOR THE Icing

Directions

1. In a medium bowl, combine the ingredients for icing, mix until smooth, and drizzle on top while cake is still warm.

THE NEXT DAY, THE FINAL ROUND APPROACHES . . .

BEFORE WE BEGIN, I HAVE A FEW MORE SURPRISES FOR EACH TEAM.

FAMILY MEMBERS HAVE BEEN FLOWN IN TO ASSIST THE CONTESTANTS IN THE KITCHENS!

THE FINAL CHALLENGE IS SIMPLE. CREATE A DESSERT TABLE. THE THEME IS A BIRTHDAY PARTY!

ANOTHER TWIST?

ALL FORMER CONTESTANTS ARE BACK!

I HAVE ALREADY CHOSEN WHICH SIDES THEY WILL BE ON, SO YOU'D BUTTER GET RIGHT TO IT THEN!

I'M SO HAPPY YOU MADE IT!

WE **CANNOT** LET HER WIN.

YOU HAVE FIVE HOURS.

BAKE ME PROUD!

MAYBE WE COULD START SETTING THE TABLE?

SURE!

WE CAN START ON SOME FLOWERS FOR A CAKE, I GUESS?

OKAY.

SHOULD WE HAVE SOME KIND OF THEME?

PROBABLY?

MADISON! DON'T BE AN IDIOT! I NEEDED THAT ICING DONE **YESTERDAY!**

YES, CHEF . . .

I SWEAR THAT WAS THE ONLY THING I DID! IT WAS ALL JUST A JOKE! I KNEW I WOULD WIN ANYWAY.

WHAT ABOUT OUR CAKE? AND KURT AND CORRIE'S FLOWERS? THERE WERE NO CAMERAS IF IT WAS DONE OVERNIGHT.

LET HER GO.

NO, I WANT TO TALK TO HER.

I'M HAPPY TO ANNOUNCE THAT ROSE AND FRED ARE THIS YEAR'S *BATTER ROYALE* CHAMPIONS! YOU WILL RECEIVE HALF A MILLION DOLLARS AND A BRILLIANT BOOK DEAL!

CONGRATS, HON! I KNEW YOU COULD DO IT.

THANKS DAD!

OBVIOUSLY, IT'S A TALENT THAT COMES FROM MY SIDE.

OF COURSE, WE ARE BOTH **SO** PROUD OF YOU.

UMM, I'M NOT SO SURE ABOUT THAT, JEFF.

NO REALLY! REMEMBER THAT ONE TIME I MADE RICE PUDDING? IT WAS PRETTY GOOD!

WHAT?

MAPLE CARAMEL Sauce

MAKES 1 CUP

½ cup of sugar

½ teaspoon salt

½ cup heavy whipping cream

1 teaspoon maple syrup

Directions

1. Bring ¼ cup of water, the sugar, and salt to a boil in a small saucepan while stirring.

2. Simmer on medium to low heat, stirring occasionally until the mixture eventually turns an amber color.

3. Add the cream and reduce heat to low.

4. Keep stirring occasionally to get rid of the foam.

5. Cook to a temperature of 200°F, or until the sauce becomes thick enough to coat a spoon.

6. Transfer to a heatproof container and add the maple syrup, then allow to cool before using.

THANK YOUS:

To my fairy godmother agent, Adria Goetz
and Martin Literary Management for believing in me.

To Charlotte Greenbaum, Andrea Miller, and everyone at Abrams,
for taking my story on and helping to crank this book out,
you've made my dream come true!

To Andrew and Cat for helping produce this beast.

To John, for always being there for me and
supporting all of my weird creative whims.

To my kids, J.T. and Jason, for being my inspiration.

To the family, friends, and colleagues who supported my journey.

To Svetlana, Bianca, and Faith for the professional advice.

To everyone online, who has supported my work
and cheered me on over the years.

To Halifax and London, my two favorite cities,
and to Peggy Porschen Academy, for teaching me
how to bake and decorate cakes.

Finally, thank you to the Ontario Arts Council
for the grant support.